W9-AMO-592

The Many Faces of Max

By Katherine Del Monte • Illustrated by Susan Arena

Las muchas caras de Max

Escrito por Katherine Del Monte • Ilustrado por Susan Arena

Lectura Books
Los Angeles

Some days
I love to
be silly.

♥ ♥ ♥

Algunos días
me gusta
ser juguetón.

I'm shy
when I meet
new people.

♥ ♥ ♥

Soy tímido
cuando conozco
a gente nueva.

5

I cry when
I hurt myself.

♥ ♥ ♥

Lloro cuando
me lastimo.

I'm sad
when my family
goes away.

♥ ♥ ♥

Me siento triste
cuando mi
familia se va.

Watch out when I'm hungry.

♥ ♥ ♥

Cuidado cuando tengo hambre.

I'm joyful when my family comes back home.

♥ ♥ ♥

Estoy contento cuando mi familia regresa a casa.

Most mornings I wake up with a **smile**.

♥ ♥ ♥

Casi siempre amanezco con una **sonrisa**.

My friends make me laugh.

♥ ♥ ♥

Mis amigos me hacen reír.

It makes me happy to chase the ball.

♥ ♥ ♥

Me hace feliz perseguir la pelota.

The best feeling
in the world
is being loved.

♥ ♥ ♥

El mejor sentimiento
del mundo
es ser amado.

Copyright © 2012 Lectura Books
All rights reserved
First edition

Publisher's Cataloging-In-Publication Data
(Prepared by The Donohue Group, Inc.)

Del Monte, Katherine.
  The many faces of Max / by Katherine Del Monte ; illustrated by Susan Arena =
Las muchas caras de Max / por Katherine Del Monte ; ilustrado por Susan Arena.

    p. : ill. ; cm.

  Bilingual. Parallel text in English and Spanish.
  Summary: Shares how Max the dog uses various facial expressions to show how
he is feeling.
  ISBN: 978-1-60448-017-7 (hardcover)
  ISBN: 978-1-60448-025-2 (pbk.)

  1. Facial expression--Juvenile literature. 2. Emotions in animals--
Juvenile literature. 3. Dogs--Juvenile literature. 4. Facial expression.
5. Emotions in animals. 6. Dogs. 7. Spanish language materials--Bilingual.
I. Arena, Susan. II. Title. III. Title: Muchas caras de Max

BF593 .D45 2011
153.69 [E]   2011937639

Lectura Books
1107 Fair Oaks Ave., Suite 225, South Pasadena, CA 91030
1-877-LECTURA (532-8872) • lecturabooks.com

Printed in Singapore